KOZO the SPARROW

Allen Say

CLARION BOOKS
An Imprint of HarperCollins*Publishers*

For Miki

The three bad boys were busy.

I always ran when I saw them, but this time,

I wanted to see what they had stolen.

Toad Boy had something in his hand . . . a baby bird.

Was it still alive?

When Toad Boy poked at it, it twitched. Just then I wanted the tiny baby more than anything in the world.

"What are you going to do with it?" I asked from a distance.

The bullies stared at me. Only the village policeman talked to them—always to chase them away.

"Why do you care?" Toad Boy said.

"What do you want for it?" I asked.

"What've you got?"

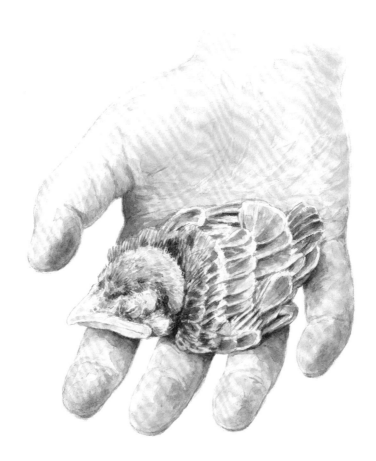

"I have a horseshoe magnet," I said.
They kept staring at me.

"And a spinning top," I quickly added.
Toad Boy said nothing.

"And nine marbles, too!"
I shouted.

He turned away.

"He has an American baseball," the bully in a white cap said.

"Bring all of it—and the baseball," Toad Boy said.

"It's not mine. My father's friend gave it to him," I tried not to whine.

"Go find a cat," Toad Boy ordered his buddies.

I gave them my treasures.

The bird was still alive, and that made me forget how angry my father was going to be. I held the baby in the nest of my hands. The yellow beak opened and closed.
Maybe he was taking his last breaths.
The bullies laughed behind me.

When I got home, my mother cried, "A baby sparrow!
Poor thing must have fallen out of the nest. Only the mother
bird can feed it. It may not live much longer . . ."

"Nothing can save that creature!" Father shouted.

"It wasn't your fault," I whispered. "You lost your mother."

Let me be your mother!
I know how swallows feed their babies—
I need a beak!

I put the baby in a box and rushed to the kitchen.

I didn't know what I was looking for until I saw a drinking straw—could this be a long beak?

I put a bit of cold rice at the tip of the straw and waved it
close to the baby's head.

Chit-chit-chit, I clicked my tongue—I clicked and waved,
clicked and waved.

Finally, the baby opened his yellow beak the way little children catch the falling snow.

And just like a mother bird I put the rice in his throat and he swallowed. Quickly, another bite, then water like raindrops, *tap, tap, tap*.

"Good boy, Kozo!" I cried. A sparrow named Little Boy.

Maybe it was a girl bird, but I wasn't sure.

I made a nest of yarn in the box and covered it with a piece of cloth.

"Good night, Kozo."

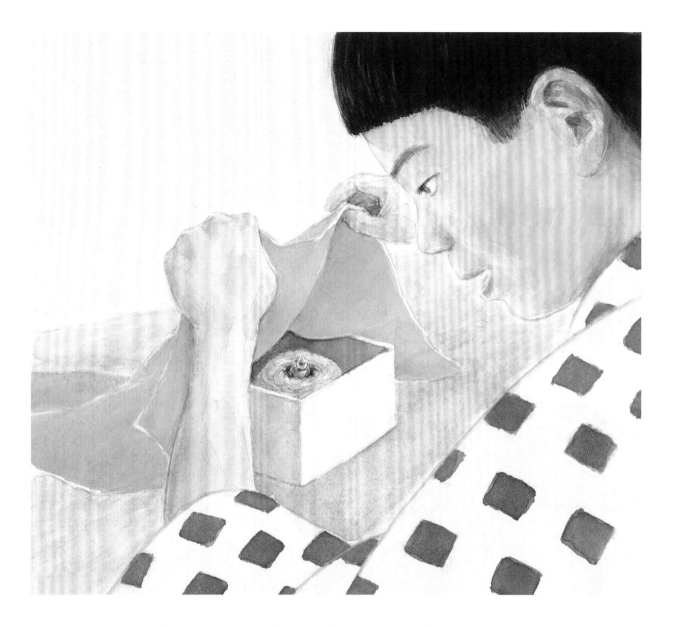

In the morning, I lifted the cover and two shining eyes peeked back.

Kozo's beak opened like a flower.

Good morning!

I fed him until it was time to go to school.

"Stay in bed and be a good boy," I told him. "I'll be back as soon as I can."

All morning I thought of Kozo.

Why did everybody raise their hands so much?

Why did the teacher speak so slowly?

Kozo was all alone and hungry . . .

And after the last lesson, there was a rehearsal for a play I'd forgotten about. I had the main part, the warrior monk named Benkei. Instead of reading my fierce lines, I burst out crying.

"What's wrong?" the teacher asked.

"I have to feed Kozo," I sobbed.

"Do you have a new brother?"

"No. My baby sparrow . . . he has to eat soon or he's going to die!"

"He has a baby sparrow!" the whole class giggled.

"Off you go then—hurry!" said the teacher.

Kozo was alive.

He twitched his wings and opened his beak.

He was happy to see me!

Every day, I ran home and played with Kozo.

The morning he sat on my shoulder at breakfast,
Mother gave me money for a cage.

I bought a beautiful one for songbirds, made of bamboo.

Kozo took baths in sand and water and spread his wings
in a sunny place until his feathers were fluffy.

"Smart boy, Kozo! You know everything already!

I wish I could splash in the bath like you."

I was sure to clean up the mess before Father could see.

I rolled a ball of yarn toward Kozo.

When he pecked at it and knew the yarn was soft, he hopped on it.

I pulled at a loose thread and he lost balance.

He fell and hopped back on again and again, cheeping all the while. Maybe I was teaching him to fly!

He was curious about *everything*.

I dangled a cold noodle like a wiggly worm, and when he finally got his beak on it, he looked surprised.

It was good to eat. I pulled and he pulled back.

We played tug-of-war.

When Kozo heard my footsteps, he chirped and beat his wings until I let him out of the cage.

He was quiet for everyone else.

One day, I came home and didn't hear Kozo.

His cage was empty, and the window was open.

My heart beat faster when I saw my mother and the woman from next door in the garden.

"What happened?" I asked.

"I was just showing your bird and he hopped out the window . . ."

"No! No! No!" I shouted.

"Kozo! Kozo!"

Calling his name and clicking my tongue, I rushed
from bush to bush, around the shrubs, tree to tree.

Suddenly, I felt him land on my head, chirping away.

He beat his wings and took a bath in my hair!

I raised my hand and he hopped on my finger.

I didn't speak to Mother all afternoon.

"Clip his wings," Father said.

"Never!" I shouted.

He shrugged and went back to his paper.

After the school play was over, the teacher came for a home visit.

She was very impressed with Kozo and asked me to bring him to school.

"But they will scare Kozo," I said.

"I will watch the children," the teacher promised.

At school the next morning, I let Kozo perch on my finger
and gave him breadcrumbs from my hand and mouth.

Everybody wanted to feed him.

They crowded around me and tried to touch Kozo.

He fluttered and bumped into walls and windows.

Everybody laughed and chased him until he shrank into
a corner and trembled with fright.

"Stop it! Stop it!" I yelled.

After I gently put him back in the cage, the teacher told me
I could take him home.

Outside the gate, the bullies were waiting.

I threw off the cage cover, dropped my school
bag, and ran.

I ran as fast as I could,

I ran as far as I could.

Then I stopped.

Author's Note

This story began when I was eight. World War II had ended and my family had moved to a town on a far corner of Kyushu, Japan. I was a city boy in a remote place where bullies chased me in the streets.

I was put in Morita Sensei's class in a local grammar school. She first appeared in *The Bicycle Man*, a story based on a sports day event there in the spring of 1946. Kozo came into my life soon afterward. He grew up as he does in the book, and I took him to class and caused a ruckus. All this happened. But from where Kozo and I leave the school is a story I've turned in my head for over seventy-six years.

When *The Bicycle Man* was published in the fall of 1982, I packed my suitcase with copies of the book and returned to the harbor town for a class reunion. Morita Sensei and nearly half of my old classmates attended—we hadn't seen each other in thirty-five years. They stared at my graying hair: "Look what America did to him!" Then they talked about Kozo. How well they remembered him! But as I handed them each a copy of *The Bicycle Man*, the banquet fell silent. Suddenly, I was a foreigner who had written a book they couldn't read, and my drawings awoke no memories in them. Sensei looked away.

Today, I know that they had forgotten the special sports day so as not be reminded of the war. And had I stayed in Japan all my life, perhaps I also might have forgotten the amazing American bicycle rider. But not Kozo.

Allen Say

Clarion Books is an imprint of HarperCollins Publishers.

Kozo the Sparrow

ISBN 978-0-06-324846-5

The artist used pencil, a dip pen and brush, and watercolor
on paper to create the illustrations for this book.
Design by Whitney Leader-Picone
23 24 25 26 27   RTLO   10 9 8 7 6 5 4 3 2 1

First Edition